Gutman, Dan.

Mr. Burke is
berserk!

$13.55

DATE			

Mr. Burke Is Berserk!

Pictures by
Jim Paillot

Dan Gutman

HARPER

An Imprint of HarperCollinsPublishers

To Emma

Mr. Burke Is Berserk!

Text copyright © 2012 by Dan Gutman

Illustrations copyright © 2012 by Jim Paillot

www.harpercollinschildrens.com

Library of Congress Cataloging-in-Publication Data

Gutman, Dan.

  Mr. Burke is berserk! / Dan Gutman ; pictures by Jim Paillot. — 1st ed.

     p.   cm. — (My weirder school ; #4)

  ISBN 978-0-06-196923-2 (lib. bdg.) — ISBN 978-0-06-196922-5 (pbk. bdg.)

  [1. Buried treasure—Fiction.   2. Gold—Fiction.   3. Schools—Fiction.   4. Humorous stories.]   I. Paillot, Jim, ill.   II. Title.

PZ7.G9846Mom 2012   2011019377

[Fic]—dc23   CIP

                                                                                     AC

Typography by Joel Tippie

12 13 14 15 16   CG/BR   10 9 8 7 6 5 4 3 2 1

❖

First Edition

Contents

The Big Race

My name is A.J. and I hate ice cream.

Actually, that's not true. I *love* ice cream. In fact, it's one of my favorite things in the world. I was just pulling your leg there.

No, I wasn't doing that either. If I was pulling your leg, I would actually be taking your leg and *pulling* on it. Why would anybody want to pull on a leg? That's a weird thing to do.*

Speaking of weird things, last week the weirdest thing in the history of the world happened. When I got to school, our groundskeeper, Mr. Burke, was sitting out in the playground on a riding lawn mower.

Well, that's not the weird part, because Mr. Burke sits on a riding lawn mower all the time. The weird part was that right next to him was our principal, Mr. Klutz. He was sitting on *another* lawn mower.

All the kids gathered around to see what was going on. I went over to my

---

*What are you looking down here for? The story is up *there*, dumbhead!

friends Ryan, Michael, Neil, and Alexia.

"What's going on?" I asked.

"Mr. Klutz and Mr. Burke are going to have a lawn mower race," said Michael, who never ties his shoes.

"The first one to reach the monkey bars wins," said Ryan, who will eat anything, even stuff that isn't food.

"Lawn mower races *rock*," said Alexia, who is a girl but is cool anyway.

"The loser has to pay the winner a dollar," said Neil, who we call the nude kid even though he wears clothes.

Mr. Klutz and Mr. Burke revved the motors of their lawn mowers and glared at each other.

"Get ready to *lose*, pardner!" shouted Mr. Burke. "Ah reckon Ah'm a-gonna give you a whuppin' you'll never forget."

He talks funny. He had a toothpick in his mouth, too. What's up with that?

"Kiss my grass!" yelled Mr. Klutz. "You're going *down*, Mr. Burke!"

That's when Andrea Young, this annoying girl with curly brown hair, came over. She was with her equally annoying crybaby friend Emily.

"Hi, Arlo!" said Andrea. She calls me by my real name because she knows I don't like it.

I didn't say hello to Andrea because I knew the guys would start teasing me and saying I was in love with her.

"They shouldn't have dangerous races and gamble on school property," Andrea told us. "It sets a bad example for children."

"I agree," said Emily, who agrees with everything Andrea says.

"Can you possibly be more boring?" asked Alexia.

Andrea stuck out her tongue at Alexia. Alexia stuck out her tongue at Andrea.

5

Emily stuck out her tongue at Alexia. Alexia stuck out her tongue at Emily.

Whenever somebody says something mean to you, always stick out your tongue at them. That's the first rule of being a kid.

"I'm not boring," Andrea said. "I just don't like violence."

"What do you have against violins?" I asked.

Everybody laughed even though I didn't say anything funny.

"Not violins, Arlo!" Andrea said, rolling her eyes. "Violence!"

Oh. Why can't a truckload of violins fall on Andrea's head?

Our gym teacher, Miss Small, came

running out in front of the lawn mowers.
She was carrying a big flag.

"On your mark," she yelled, "get set . . .
GO!"

She waved the flag. Mr. Klutz and Mr.
Burke took off.*

*Ha-ha, made you look down!

A Seesaw Battle

The lawn mower race was hilarious, because lawn mowers go *really* slow. I mean, I can *walk* faster than those things. It was like watching a turtle race. But it

was still exciting, and everybody was yelling and screaming.

"Put the pedal to the metal, Mr. Klutz!"

"You can beat him, Mr. Burke!"

We all walked alongside the lawn mowers so we could see who was winning. First Mr. Klutz took the lead. Then Mr. Burke took the lead. Then Mr. Klutz was ahead. Then Mr. Burke was ahead.

"This is a real seesaw battle!" shouted Ryan.

"Are they going to fight on the seesaws?" I asked. "That would be *cool*!"

After about a million hundred minutes, the lawn mowers reached the other end of the playground. Mr. Burke jumped off and touched the monkey bars first.

"Yee-ha!" he shouted. "Ah'm a-grinnin' like a weasel in a hen-house."

Mr. Klutz gave Mr. Burke a dollar. All the excitement was over, and we had to go into school to start the day. Bummer in the summer!

"Mr. Burke is weird," I said as we walked to class.

"Remember the time he grew a corn maze on the soccer field?" asked Neil.

"Remember the time he mowed big circles in the grass and told us they were made by UFOs?" asked Michael.

"Maybe Mr. Burke isn't really a grounds-keeper at all," I said. "Maybe he kidnapped the *real* groundskeeper and locked him in the equipment shed where he keeps the lawn mowers. Stuff like that happens all the time, you know."

"Stop trying to scare Emily," said Andrea.

"I'm scared!" said Emily.

"Mr. Burke probably escaped from a loony bin," said Ryan.

"Yeah," I said. "He probably snatches

kids during recess and buries them under the monkey bars."

"We've got to *do* something!" Emily shouted. Then she started freaking out and went running down the hallway.

Sheesh, get a grip! That girl will fall for *anything*.

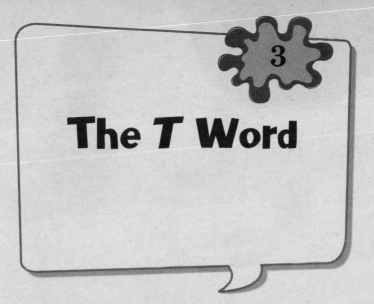

The *T* Word

The rest of us walked to class with our teacher, Mr. Granite, who is from another planet. After we put our backpacks into our cubbies and pledged the allegiance, it was time for math. But you'll never believe who poked his head into the door at that moment.

Nobody! Poking your head into a door

would hurt. But you'll never believe who poked his head into the *doorway*.

It was Mr. Klutz!

"To what do we owe the pleasure of your company?" asked Mr. Granite.

That's grown-up talk for "What are *you* doing here?"

"Remember when I went to principal camp last year?" he said. "Well, I have to go again. I just wanted to say good-bye."

"Bye!" we all said.

Principal camp sounds cool. I'll bet the principals sit around a campfire and toast marshmallows. Maybe I'll be a principal when I grow up so I can go to camp and eat toasted marshmallows.

After Mr. Klutz left, Mr. Granite went to the front of the room.

"It's time for math," he said. "Turn to page twenty-three in your—"

But he didn't get the chance to finish his sentence, because at that moment an announcement came over the loud-speaker.

"All classes please report to the all-purpose room immediately."

"Not *again*!" moaned Mr. Granite.

"Yay, no math!" I yelled.

We had to walk a million hundred miles to the all-purpose room. Along the way, we saw our art teacher, Ms. Hannah, and our music teacher, Mr. Loring. They were each pulling a rolling suitcase.

"Why did you bring suitcases to school?" Ryan asked them.

"We take them with us wherever we go," said Ms. Hannah, "because you never know when you're going to get fired."

"We like to be ready," added Mr. Loring.

Ms. Hannah and Mr. Loring are weird.

In the all-purpose room our class got to sit in the front row. But I had to sit next to annoying Andrea. Ugh, disgusting! I made sure not to let my elbow touch her elbow on the armrest so I wouldn't catch her girl germs.

The vice principal, Mrs. Jafee, was on the stage. She held up her hand and made a peace sign, which means "shut up."

"I'll be in charge while Mr. Klutz is gone," she told us. "We have a special guest who would like to speak with us today. How about a big round of applause for Mayor Hubble?"

We all clapped our hands in circles. Mayor Hubble came down the aisle with two secret service agents behind him. He was smiling, passing out buttons that said REELECT MAYOR HUBBLE, and shaking hands with everybody.

It would be cool to be the mayor. He's like the king of the town. My friend Billy who lives around the corner told me that Mayor Hubble has a limo, and a big throne at city hall. Guys carry the mayor around in a chair, and girls in bikinis feed him grapes.

Mayor Hubble climbed up on the stage. "I have bad news," he announced. "The town is broke. The government has cut

off all our money, but we still have to balance the budget."

I didn't know what he was talking about.

"Does this mean you're going to raise taxes?" asked Ms. Jafee.

"Taxes?!"

Mayor Hubble suddenly groaned, grabbed his chest, and dropped to his knees. It looked like he was gonna die.

One of his secret service agents rushed over to help the mayor. The other one leaned over to talk to Mrs. Jafee.

"Never say the *T* word in front of the mayor," he told her.

Mayor Hubble leaned into the microphone.

"I will *not* raise taxes!" he shouted. "I'm going to *lower* taxes!"

"If we don't have enough money," asked Mrs. Jafee, "shouldn't you raise, uh, the *T* word?"

"Read my lips," Mayor Hubble shouted at her. "No new taxes!"

"Why do we need to read your lips?" I asked. "You're *talking.*"

"That's just an expression, Arlo," Andrea told me, rolling her eyes.

"I don't understand," said Mrs. Jafee. "How can we get the money to balance the budget if you don't raise . . . the *T* word?"

"I have an idea," said Mrs. Roopy, our media specialist. "We could have a car wash. We could raise the money, balance the budget, and have fun all at the same time!"

"Yeah!" everybody shouted excitedly.

"No!" said Mayor Hubble.

"How about a bake sale?" asked Miss Laney, our speech teacher. "People love to buy cookies and cakes."

"No!" said Mayor Hubble.

"A raffle?" suggested our reading specialist, Mr. Macky.

"No!" said Mayor Hubble.

"Why not just close down the school?" I suggested. "That would save money. Then we could stay home and play video games all day."

All the kids cheered at my genius idea.

"No!" said Mayor Hubble. "There's only one way to balance the budget. I can tell you with just three little letters."

Three Little Letters

The three little letters were *C-U-T*.

"Cuts!" Mayor Hubble shouted into the microphone. "We need to cut the amount of money we spend so we can balance the budget!"

Just saying the word "cut" seemed to make Mayor Hubble's eyes light up with

excitement. He had a crazy look on his face, the kind of look that evil geniuses in the movies have when they explain how they're going to take over the world.

"The first things we're going to cut," Mayor Hubble told us, "are the art and music programs."

"So long," said Ms. Hannah, taking her rolling suitcase. "I'm outta here."

"Right behind you," said Mr. Loring.

"But we *love* art and music!" one of the kids shouted.

"You kids are here to *learn*," said the mayor, "not to sit around drawing pictures and singing silly songs. That's just a big waste of money."

Everybody looked really sad when Ms. Hannah and Mr. Loring walked out of the all-purpose room.

"The next things we need to cut are school supplies," said Mayor Hubble. "So from now on we're going to stop buying glue sticks, rulers, erasers, tape, and markers. You can have one pencil per classroom."

"That's off the wall!" yelled Miss Small.

"Oh, stop whining," said Mayor Hubble. "This will improve everyone's schoolwork.

If the students only have one pencil, they'll make fewer mistakes."

"What about crayons?" asked Miss Holly, our Spanish teacher.

"No more crayons," said Mayor Hubble. "You can melt down candles and make them into crayons. That will save us a lot of money."

"That's loopy!" yelled Mrs. Roopy.

The mayor pulled a piece of paper out of his pocket to remind him of the other things he was going to cut.

"Starting today," he announced, "I'm turning off the water fountains in the hallways. Do you know what the biggest waste of water in the world is? Water fountains! The water just shoots right out of them!"

"That's bizarre!" yelled Miss Lazar, our custodian.

"Oh, give me a break," Mayor Hubble said. "It's not like people *need* water to live or anything. And I know you kids just go to the water fountain when you don't want to sit in class. You're not fooling anybody."

Well, he was right about *that*.

"That's daffy!" yelled Mrs. Jafee.

"From now on," the mayor continued, "there will be no more toilet paper in the bathrooms. That stuff costs way too much money."

"You're getting rid of the toilet paper?"

shouted Alexia. "What are we supposed to use?"

"Post-it Notes," said the mayor.

"That's loony!" yelled Mrs. Cooney, the school nurse. "And disgusting!"

"From now on the teachers will have their pay cut in half," the mayor continued. "You teachers make way too much money."

Teachers get paid? That was a new one on me. I thought they just came to school every day because they had no place else to go.

"But we hardly make any money as it is!" yelled Mrs. Yonkers, our computer teacher.

"What do *you* teach?" Mayor Hubble asked Mrs. Yonkers.

"I'm the computer teacher."

"Well, you're fired," said the mayor. "I'm replacing you with a computer. A computer should be able to teach a computer class much better than a human being anyway. And computers don't whine and complain like people do."

"He's off his rocker!" yelled Mr. Docker, our science teacher.

"You crybaby teachers should be thankful you have jobs at all," said the mayor. "Oh, and I want the coffee machine and the hot tub removed from the teachers' lounge."

"We don't have a hot tub in the teachers' lounge," said Mrs. Jafee.

"You don't?" said the mayor. "Hmmm. Then put a hot tub in the teachers' lounge and then take it out. We have no money to spend on silly things like hot tubs for teachers."

"He's loco!" said Ms. Coco, the gifted and talented teacher.

Mayor Hubble was getting more and more excited as he talked about all the cuts he was going to make.

"After we get rid of the hot tub in the teachers' lounge," he said, "get rid of the tables and chairs in there and sell them on eBay."

"Do you expect the teachers to sit on the *floor*?" asked Mr. Granite.

"Yes!" said Mayor Hubble. "It will be like a picnic every day. You like picnics, don't you? Who doesn't like a picnic?"

"He's gone mad!" said Dr. Brad, the school counselor.

"Come to think of it," said the mayor, "why do you teachers need a lounge anyway? You don't have time for lounging around in hot tubs and having picnics. This is a school, not some beach resort."

"But we don't *have* a hot tub!" yelled Miss Laney, our speech teacher.

"Not anymore you won't," said the mayor. "Not after I get rid of the one we're putting in. All these cuts will help us balance the budget. And when the voters see how much money I saved, they'll vote to reelect me in November."

"Are *you* going to take a pay cut too?" asked Mrs. Jafee.

"Don't be silly," said Mayor Hubble. "I'm giving myself a raise for coming up with these great ideas to save money."

"'That makes no sense!" yelled Officer Spence, our security guard. "We *need* pencils and glue sticks and water fountains and toilet paper. We *need* tables and chairs. We need all those things that you're going to cut."

"Yeah!" shouted all the teachers.

"If Mr. Klutz was here, he would never allow any of this," said Mr. Granite.

"That's right!" shouted the teachers.

"Well, Mr. Klutz isn't here, is he?" asked Mayor Hubble. "He's at principal camp."

Everybody was really mad. And you'll never believe who poked his head into the door at that moment.

Nobody! Poking your head into doors is dumb. I thought we went over that in the last chapter.

But you'll never believe who poked his head into the *doorway*.*

It was Mr. Burke, the groundskeeper!

"Ah mowed the lawn," said Mr. Burke.

---

*No, it wasn't Mr. Klutz. Nice try though.

"You're Fired!"

"Ah trimmed the bushes. Ah been busier than a one-armed man hangin' wallpaper, and Ah am plum tuckered out. What do you want me to do next?"

"Next?" asked Mayor Hubble. "The next thing you can do is go home. There's no money in the budget for a groundskeeper anymore. So you're fired. Have a nice day."

I think that was the moment when Mr. Burke went berserk.

The Class Pencil

None of us could believe that Mr. Burke had been fired. Who would mow the lawn? Who would trim the bushes? Who would rake the leaves in the fall and shovel the snow in the winter?

Mr. Burke didn't say a word. He just

stood up and walked slowly out the doorway.

When we got back to class, I looked out the window and saw Mr. Burke sitting all by himself on the monkey bars in the playground. It was sad.

"Okay, it's time for math," said Mr. Granite. "Get out your pencils and turn to page twenty-three in your math books. Do the first problem and write the answer in your notebook."

Ugh. I hate math.

"I don't have a pencil," said Ryan.

"Me neither," said Michael.

"My pencil is gone!" said Neil the nude kid.

"Somebody stole my pencil, too!" said Alexia.

"Somebody took *all* of our pencils!" said Andrea.

It was true! All of our pencils were gone. Our glue sticks, tape, erasers, and rulers were gone, too.

"Somebody stole our stuff!" I shouted.

"Who would steal school supplies?" asked Andrea.

"Mayor Hubble!" said Mr. Granite. "He's probably going to sell our school supplies on eBay so he can balance the budget."

"Wow," I said, "he didn't waste any time."

"Mayor Hubble is *mean*!" said Emily.

"That may be true, but we still have to

do math," said Mr. Granite. "There's one pencil on my desk. We'll just have to share the class pencil."

"Can I use the class pencil *first*?" asked Little Miss Perfect. "I already know the answer to the first problem."

Andrea always knows the answer to *every* problem. I hate her.

"I want the class pencil first!" I shouted. "Please, Mr. Granite?"

I didn't even want the dumb pencil. I just didn't want Little Miss Know-It-All to get it.

"Andrea and A.J. may *share* the class pencil," said Mr. Granite. "Then pass it down to the next person."

"Oooooh!" Ryan said. "A.J. and Andrea are going to share the class pencil. They must be in *love!*"

"When are you gonna get married?" asked Michael.

If those guys weren't my best friends, I would hate them.

Andrea snatched the pencil from Mr. Granite before I could get it. I grabbed the other end of the pencil.

"I get to use the class pencil *first*, Arlo!" said Andrea.

"No," I shouted at her, "we're supposed to share it."

"Me!"

"No, me!"

"Both of you! Knock it—"

Mr. Granite didn't get the chance to finish his sentence. Because at that moment the weirdest thing in the history of the world happened.

SNAP!

The class pencil broke in half.

"Look what you did, Arlo!" shouted

Andrea. "You broke the class pencil!"

"I didn't break it," I shouted back at her. "*You* broke it!"

"I did not!"

"Did too."

"Now we can't do math," said Michael.

"Yay!" said Ryan. "No math!"

"Mr. Granite, Arlo broke the class pencil on purpose so he wouldn't have to do math!" Andrea yelled.

"I did not!"

"Did too!"

Andrea started hitting me, and I hit her back.

"Stop!" shouted Mr. Granite. "I will not have violence in my classroom!"

"What do you have against violins?" I asked.

"Not violins, Arlo!" said Andrea, rolling her eyes. "Violence!"

"Oh. That sounds a lot like violins to me."

"Forget the class pencil," said Mr. Granite. "We'll use the whiteboard. You kids will *not* get out of doing math *this* time."

I had to admit that breaking the class pencil to get out of doing math wasn't a bad idea. I wish I had thought of it. But that gave me another idea.

"Mr. Granite," I said, "can I go get a drink of water?"

"Mayor Hubble turned off the water

fountains," he replied. "Remember?"

"Oh yeah," I said. "May I go to the boys' room?"

"Do you *really* have to go to the boys' room, A.J.?" Mr. Granite asked me. "Or are you just trying to get out of math?"

"I really have to go," I lied.

"Well, okay," said Mr. Granite. "Here, take some Post-it Notes with you."

I was about to walk out the doorway when the weirdest thing in the history of the world happened.

Brrrring! Brrrring! Brrrring!

It was the recess bell!

Yay! No math!

It was the greatest moment of my life.

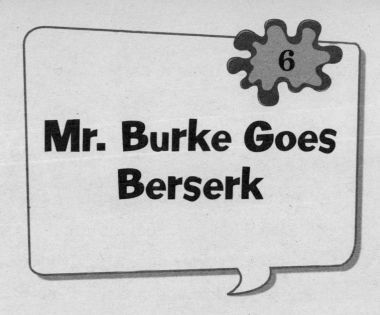

Mr. Burke Goes Berserk

When we went out to the playground for recess, two big guys were there.* They were sawing off the bottoms of the monkey bars. When they finished, they picked

---

*Hey, do you want to know the surprise ending to the story? Well, I'm not going to tell you. So nah-nah-nah boo-boo on you.

the whole thing up and started carrying it away.

"Where are you taking our monkey bars?" I asked.

"To Rent-A-Monkey Bars," one of the guys replied. "You can rent anything."

They also took away our swings, slides, climbing wall, kickballs, volleyball nets, soccer goals, and jump ropes. They even took the tetherball pole out of the ground! Then they threw all that stuff into a big truck and drove away.

We were sad. There was nothing to do. What fun is recess when you have nothing to play with?

"Mayor Hubble is *mean*," said Andrea. And for once I agreed with her.

We wandered around the playground until we saw Mr. Burke coming out of the equipment shed. He had something in his hand.

"Why is he still here?" asked Alexia. "Mayor Hubble fired him."

"What's he holding?" asked Ryan.

"It looks like a . . . chain saw," said Andrea.

A CHAIN SAW?!

We all started freaking out.

"Mr. Burke is crazy!" I yelled.

"He must have snapped," yelled Neil the nude kid.

"He's going to kill everybody in the school!" yelled Ryan.

"It will be like that movie *The Texas*

Chain Saw Massacre!" yelled Michael.

Mr. Burke pulled a cord to start up the chain saw, and it made a loud noise like a motorcycle.

"We've got to *do* something!" yelled Emily.

We were about to run inside and warn the teachers when Mr. Burke went over to the biggest bush in the playground.

"Wait a minute," said Andrea. "He's not going to kill anybody. He's going to trim the bushes!"

Andrea was right, as usual. Mr. Burke started cutting the side of the big bush with the chain saw. He carefully cut into one side and then he went around to cut the other side.

"Why is he trimming—" Emily started to say.

"He's not trimming it!" Andrea said. "He's making a *sculpture*. He's making a bush sculpture!"

She was right again. And Mr. Burke wasn't just making *any* sculpture. As he cut into the bush with the chain saw, we could see that he was making a sculpture of a *person*. And as he continued cutting, we could see that the person wasn't just *any* person.

"It's . . . Mayor Hubble!" shouted Alexia.

She was right, too. The bush looked just like the mayor.

"Mr. Burke is weird," said Ryan.

Andrea had on her worried face, so

I knew she was going to say something about her mother the psychologist.

"I'm worried," she said. "My mother is a psychologist. She would say that Mr. Burke is obsessed with Mayor Hubble. He needs to move on with his life and get a new job."

"I agree," said Emily, who always agrees with everything Andrea says.

Mr. Burke put the finishing touches on his sculpture. Then he put the chain saw back into the shed and came out with a shovel.

"What's he doing *now*?" asked Neil the nude kid.

Mr. Burke went over to where the monkey bars used to be. Then he started digging a hole in the ground with the shovel.

"See? It's like I told you," I said. "He must be digging up the bodies of the kids he murdered."

"Arlo, stop trying to scare Emily," said Andrea.

"I'm scared!" said Emily.

"Maybe he'll dig up some zombies," said Ryan. "They'll come back to life and chase us around the playground."

"And if they catch us, they'll eat our brains," said Michael. "I saw that in a movie once."

Emily started freaking out.

"Zombies don't eat brains, dumbhead," said Alexia.

"*Cannibal* zombies do," I told her. "Especially cannibal zombies from outer space."

"We've got to *do* something!" yelled Emily, and then she went running away.

Sheesh, what a crybaby.

The rest of us kept watching Mr. Burke digging with the shovel. First he would dig one hole and then he would dig another hole nearby. And then another one.

"I think he's looking for something," said Ryan.

"Maybe he's digging up the Underground Railroad," I suggested.

We learned about that in class with Mr. Granite.

"The Underground Railroad wasn't underground, Arlo!" Andrea said, rolling her eyes.

"Then why did they call it the 'Underground Railroad'?" I asked.

"Because it was *hidden*," Andrea said. "They didn't want people to know about it."

"Your *face* should be hidden," I told Andrea. "Then we wouldn't have to look at it."

"Oh, snap!" said Ryan.

Andrea was trying to think of something mean to say to me. But she never got the chance. Because that's when the weirdest thing in the history of the world happened. Mr. Burke's shovel hit something sharp.

PING!

He must have broken off a piece of rock. He got down on his hands and knees and picked it up. He was looking at it carefully. Then he took a magnifying glass out of his pocket and looked through it. He turned the rock over and over in his hand.

And then he stood up and yelled . . .

"It's GOLD!"

Gold Fever

"Gold!" shouted Ryan.

"Gold!!" shouted Michael.

"Gold!!!" shouted Neil the nude kid.

"GOLD!!!!" I shouted.

Just in case you were wondering, we were all shouting "Gold."

Kids from every corner of the

playground came running over to see what was going on.

"Mr. Burke found gold!"

"Mr. Burke found gold!!"

"MR. BURKE FOUND GOLD!!!"

Just in case you were wondering, lots

of kids were talking about how Mr. Burke found gold. Everybody crowded around him as he held up the chunk of gold.

"Well, Ah'll be dogged," Mr. Burke said. "Mah great-great-grandpappy lived over yonder back in '48. He told me there was a heap a gold left in the ground after the big gold rush ended. And Ah reckon it was right here!"

Mrs. Jafee came running out to the playground.

"What's all the fuss about?" she asked.

"Mr. Burke found a piece of gold where the monkey bars used to be," I told her.

"Ah always figgered there wuz gold down there," he said, "but Ah couldn't git at it on account a them dang monkey bars. Is it okay with y'all if Ah do a little diggin' out here?"

"You betcha!" said Mrs. Jafee. "Dig, baby, dig!"

Our reading specialist, Mr. Macky, came running out of the school. He was pushing a wheelbarrow.

"Did somebody say *gold*?" he asked, all excited.

"Where did you get a wheelbarrow?" Ryan asked Mr. Macky.

"From Rent-A-Wheelbarrow," said Mr. Macky. "You can rent anything."

Suddenly, the other teachers came running out of the school: Ms. Coco, Miss

Holly, Mr. Docker, Miss Small—all of them! They were wearing overalls and miner's helmets. Some of them were carrying pickaxes, shovels, and pans. I guess they rented them.

"Yee-ha!" they were all shouting. "Gold!"

"Uh, don't any of you have classes to teach?" asked Andrea.

"Classes?" shouted our librarian, Mrs. Roopy. "Who cares about classes? There's gold in them thar hills!"

"And Ah'm a-fixin' to fetch me some, dagnabit," said our speech teacher, Miss Laney.

"Yee-ha!" shouted Mr. Granite.

"Why is everybody suddenly talking

like it's the Wild West?" I asked.

"'Cause we got the gold fever, young feller!" said Mr. Macky. "It drives a man crazy, Ah tell you! *Crazy!*"

"Ah'm crazier than a run-over coon!" shouted our health teacher, Ms. Leakey.

"Ah'm crazier than popcorn on a hot stove!" shouted Mr. Granite.

"Yee-ha!" shouted Ms. Coco.

Grown-ups are weird.

The teachers started digging holes all over the place and saying words I never heard of, like "tarnation" and "varmint" and "ornery." Me and the other kids just watched them. At least it was better than going to class.

"Ah found me a nugget, y'all!" Miss Holly suddenly shouted. "Yee-ha!"

"A chicken nugget?" I asked.

"No, a *gold* nugget!"

That's funny. I always thought nuggets came from chickens. We all gathered around to look at Miss Holly's nugget.

"Look at the way it shines!" she said.

"That there nugget is as purty as a snake on stilts!" said Mrs. Roopy.

"Ah reckon this may be the biggest gold strike in over a hundred years," said Mr. Burke.

The teachers let out a big "yee-ha" and started digging all over the place with even more excitement.

"Ah found one, too!" shouted Miss Small.

"So did Ah!" said Mr. Granite.

They were all uncovering gold. That's when a big black car pulled up to the playground. And you'll never believe who got out of it.

It was Mayor Hubble! And he was coming over.

Suddenly, all the teachers stopped digging. Mayor Hubble was staring at the teachers. The teachers were staring at Mayor Hubble. The kids were staring at the teachers and Mayor Hubble. Everybody was staring at each other. You could hear a pin drop.*

I was sure Mayor Hubble was going to tell them to stop digging and go back to class. But he didn't.

"Dig!" he hollered. "Keep digging!"

---

*Not really, but that's what everybody says when it's quiet. Nobody knows why.

Gilver

When I got to school the next day, the front door was locked. I went around to the playground, and it was filled with teachers. They were digging holes with shovels, pickaxes, and all kinds of mining equipment.

I met up with the guys and Alexia. Mrs. Roopy came by on a donkey.

"Where did you get a donkey?" Alexia asked her.

"It's not a donkey," Mrs. Roopy said. "It's a burro. His name is Jose."

"Where did you get a burro?" Michael asked.

"From Rent-A-Burro," she said. "You can rent anything."

As we got closer, we saw the weirdest thing in the history of the world. Mr. Macky, Mr. Burke, Mr. Docker, and Officer Spence all had long beards on their faces! None of them had beards the day before.

"How did you grow a beard so fast?" Ryan asked Mr. Macky.

"It's the gold fever!" he replied, a crazy look in his eyes. "It does that to a man."

We sat and watched the teachers digging. They were all shouting "Yee-ha" and calling each other "pardner." That's when annoying Andrea and Emily came over.

"This is terrible!" Andrea said. "The teachers should be inside the school helping us learn things, not out here digging for gold."

"That's right," said Emily.

What is their problem?

"Can you possibly be more boring?" asked Alexia.

"Yeah, take a chill pill," I told Andrea. "We get a day off from school."

Mr. Burke seemed to know a lot about gold mining, and he was telling the teachers where to dig and what to do.

"Ah reckon we need to dig a deeper hole to git at the gold," he told them. "Fetch me the dynamite, fellers!"

"They're going to blow a hole in the playground?" asked Andrea. "That sounds dangerous. Is violence really necessary?"

"What do violins have to do with it?" I asked.

"Not 'violins,' Arlo! 'Violence'!"

Mr. Burke and Mr. Macky dug a deep hole where the monkey bars used to be and put sticks of dynamite in there. Then they stretched a wire from the hole to the other end of the playground.

"Y'all cover yer ears now," Mr. Burke hollered. Then he yelled "Fire in the hole!" and pushed down on this handle thing that looked like a bicycle pump. We all covered our ears.

BOOOOOOOOOOOOOOOOOM!

There was a *huge* blast. Rocks and dirt went flying all over the place. It was awesome. We got to see it live and in person. You should have been there!

"WOW," we all said, which is "MOM" upside down.

Blowing stuff up is *cool*. There should be a TV channel that shows nothing but stuff being blown up all day long.

The explosion blew a giant hole in the ground. The teachers all ran over yelling "Yee-ha." They climbed into the hole with their shovels and picks.

"You kids wanna come down into the mine with me and poke around?" Mr. Burke asked us.

"Yeah!" said me and the guys and Alexia.

"I don't want to get my school clothes dirty," said Andrea.

"Me neither," said Emily.

"Can you possibly be more boring?" asked Alexia.

The rest of us climbed into the mine with Mr. Burke. It was dark down there, but some of the teachers had lights on their helmets, so we could see.

They were digging for a long time, but nobody found any gold. And then Mr. Burke suddenly hit something sharp with his shovel.

"Ah think Ah found somethin'!" he said.

"Is it gold?" I asked.

"No."

"Is it silver?" asked Alexia.

"No," Mr. Burke said as he looked at a shiny thing in his hand. "It's even *more* valuable than gold and silver. It's . . . gilver!"

"Gilver?" asked Ryan. "I never heard of gilver."

"What's gilver?" asked Neil the nude kid.

"Gilver is a combination of gold 'n' silver," Mr. Burke said excitedly.

"Yee-ha!" shouted Mr. Macky. "It's more valuable than gold. It's more valuable than silver. It's gilver!"

"Gilver!!"

"GILVER!!!"

In case you were wondering, all the teachers were shouting "Gilver."

"This place is filled with the stuff!" said Mr. Burke. "It's a bonanza!"

"We hit pay dirt!" shouted Mr. Macky, jumping up and down and clicking his heels together. "There must be *millions* of dollars' worth of gilver down here!"

"Billions!" shouted Miss Small.

"Trillions!" shouted Mr. Granite.

"Do you have any idea what this means

for our school?" said Mrs. Jafee. "We can bring back the art and music programs!"

"We can buy new computers and SMART Boards for every classroom!" shouted Mrs. Yonkers.

"We can turn the water fountains back on!" shouted Ms. Leakey.

"We can buy toilet paper for the bathroom!" shouted Miss Lazar.

"Yee-ha!" the rest of the teachers shouted.

All our problems were solved.

The Gold Rush

The teachers filled bag after bag with gilver and carried the bags out of the hole. Mr. Burke told us not to say a word about the gilver to anybody.

But it didn't matter. Thanks to all the yelling and shouting, word got out. Five minutes later, people with overalls and hard hats and shovels were streaming into the playground from all directions. Some of them came on dogsleds. Some were in covered wagons. I guess they rented them.

The next thing we knew, the playground was filled with tents and people making campfires, cooking vittles, and playing harmonicas. It was a real Kodak moment.

"Yee-ha!" one guy said. "Ah'm hankerin' to git me a heap of that gilver!"

"Hey, we were here first, you no-good rascal!" said Mr. Macky. "It's *our* gilver!"

"Finders keepers!" said another guy.

"This is a public school, you varmint, so it's public property."

It looked like a fight was going to break out. But that's when the weirdest thing in the history of the world happened.

"Channel 7 News is on its way!"

"Channel 7 News is on its way!!"

"CHANNEL 7 NEWS IS ON ITS WAY!!!"

In case you were wondering, everybody was saying that Channel 7 News was on its way.

"TV? Cameras?" shrieked Andrea. "How does my hair look?"

"EEEEEEEEK! We're going to be famous!" shrieked Emily.

Sure enough, a few minutes later a big

van pulled up with **CHANNEL 7 NEWS** written on the side. And you'll never believe who got out of the van.

It was Mrs. Lilly, this reporter who helped us make a newspaper about our school!

Some guys from the news van set up the equipment, and Mrs. Lilly stood next to Mr. Burke.

"This is Mrs. Lilly, of Channel 7 News," she said into a microphone. "I'm reporting live from Ella Mentry School, where gilver—a rare combination of gold and silver—has been found in the playground. With me is Mr. Burke, the school grounds-keeper. You were the one who discovered

the gilver, Mr. Burke. Tell me, how do you feel right now?"

"Ah feel like Ah could eat corn on the cob through a picket fence," Mr. Burke said.

"I beg your pardon?" asked Mrs. Lilly.

"What Ah mean is, right now Ah could just about hit a bull's backside with a handful of banjos."

"I'm sorry; I don't understand," said

Mrs. Lilly.

"All Ah'm saying is, Ah feel like Ah could bluff a buzzard off a meat wagon right now."

"Huh?" said Mrs. Lilly. "I have no idea what you're talking about."

"What's a matter, ma'am?" asked Mr. Burke. "Don'tcha speak English?"

Mrs. Lilly was going to ask Mr. Burke more questions, but you'll never believe in a million hundred years who came running in front of the camera at that moment.

I'm not gonna tell you.

Okay, okay, I'll tell you. But you have to read the next chapter first. So nah-nah-nah boo-boo on you.

10

Violins Are Bad for Children

It was Mayor Hubble!

He grabbed the microphone from Mrs. Lilly. His secret service agents shoved Mr. Burke away from the camera.

"I'm happy to announce," said the mayor, "that all the gold and gilver found on school property belongs to the city. We will use it to balance the budget blah blah blah blah create new jobs blah blah blah blah fix the roads blah blah blah blah cut taxes blah blah blah blah this great country blah blah blah blah and furthermore blah blah blah blah how long is this going to go on blah blah blah blah wake me up when it's over blah blah blah blah . . ."

He yammered on for about a million hundred hours. I thought I was gonna die of old age.

"In conclusion," the mayor finally said, "vote for *me* on Election Day. Thank you."

Mrs. Lilly and the Channel 7 guys turned off their camera, packed up their gear, and drove away.

"Okay, the show's over," said Mayor Hubble. "Everybody go home now. I'll take care of this gilver. And all you teachers, get back to class! You should be ashamed of yourselves."

The secret service agents started to load

the bags of gold and gilver into the trunk of Mayor Hubble's limo.

The teachers were sad. They had worked really hard to dig up the gold and gilver. Now Mayor Hubble was taking it away. We wouldn't be able to fix up the school. We wouldn't be able to bring back the art and music programs. We wouldn't have any toilet paper.

Bummer in the summer! This was the worst thing to happen since TV Turnoff Week.

We all started walking back into school. That's when the most amazing thing in the history of the world happened. In the distance, at the other end of the playground, a tall, mysterious stranger appeared. He was walking toward us in slow motion.

And he was bald.

It was Mr. Klutz!

"Mr. Klutz!"

"Mr. Klutz!!"

"MR. KLUTZ!!!"

In case you were wondering, everybody was shouting "Mr. Klutz." He stopped about twenty feet from Mayor Hubble.

"Klutz!" said the mayor. "What in blazes are *you* doing here?"

"They let me out of principal camp early," said Mr. Klutz. "The jig is up,

Mayor. Give us back that gold and gilver. It doesn't belong to you."

"Who's gonna *make* me?" the mayor asked.

"*Oooooooooooooooooo!*" everybody said.

"Ah reckon Ah am," said Mr. Klutz. "Because yer gettin' too big fer yer britches."

"*Oooooooooooooooooo!*"

"Smile when you say that," said the mayor.

Mayor Hubble looked at Mr. Klutz. Mr. Klutz looked at Mayor Hubble. All the kids and teachers were looking at Mr. Klutz and Mayor Hubble. Nobody was saying anything. A tumbleweed rolled by.

"That gilver belongs to mah teachers and mah school," said Mr. Klutz. "Ah reckon you're tryin' to steal it and keep it for yourself."

"Yer lyin' like a rug, Klutz," said Mayor Hubble.

"And yer so crooked, you could swallow nails and spit out corkscrews," said Mr. Klutz. "Just give back the gilver and nobody gets hurt."

"Nothin' doin'," said the mayor. "Ah'm

afraid this playground ain't big enough fer the both of us, Klutz."

"Ooooooooooooooooooo!"

"Then Ah'm gonna have to give you a whuppin' you'll never forget, Mayor," said Mr. Klutz, "'cause you're a bad egg."

"Ooooooooooooooooooo!"

"Ah'm gonna kick your butt so hard, they're gonna need a team of surgeons to remove mah boot!" said Mayor Hubble.*

"Ooooooooooooooooooo!"

Mr. Klutz and Mayor Hubble were *really* mad. They started walking toward each other in slow motion. It looked like

---

*It's okay to say "but," but grown-ups get mad when you say "butt." Nobody knows why.

they were about to fight.

But you'll never believe who ran out and stood between them.

It was Andrea Young! Little Miss Perfect! The Human Homework Machine!

"Stop!" Andrea shouted, holding up her hands. "There's no need to resort to violence."

"Why is everybody always talking about violins?" I asked. "Are they going to fight with musical instruments? They should fight with tubas.* That would be cool."

"Not 'violins'!" everybody shouted at me. "'Violence!'"

"Oh," I said. "Why didn't you say so?"

---

*"Tuba" spelled backwards is "a but."

Suddenly, Mr. Burke pushed his way to the front of the crowd.

"The little lady is right," he said. "Ah say we settle this the old-fashioned way: with a duel."

"A duel!"

"A duel!!"

"A DUEL!!!"

In case you were wondering, everybody was saying "A duel."

"Guns are violent, Mr. Burke," said Andrea.

"Ah ain't talkin' 'bout a duel with guns," said Mr. Burke. "Ah'm talkin' 'bout a *modern* duel . . . with cell phones!"

The Duel

Mr. Burke explained the rules of the duel to everybody. The mayor and Mr. Klutz would each write their cell phone number on a piece of paper and swap the papers. Then they would stand back-to-back. They would each walk ten paces forward. Then they would turn around, grab their cell phones, and dial each other's number as fast as possible. Whichever cell phone rang first would be the loser. The other one would get to keep all the gold and gilver.

"It's a deal," said Mayor Hubble.

"Deal," said Mr. Klutz. "Ah'm betting mah smartphone is smarter than yer smartphone."

"Ah'm warnin' ya," said the mayor, "Ah'm purty quick on the dial."

"No namby-pamby gilver rustler can out-dial me," said Mr. Klutz.

Mr. Burke told Mr. Klutz and Mayor Hubble to stand back-to-back.

"Look, their butts are touching!" I whispered.

"Quiet, Arlo!" shouted Andrea.

"Ready . . . set . . . GO!" said Mr. Burke.

Mr. Klutz and Mayor Hubble started pacing away from each other.

1 . . . 2 . . . 3 . . . 4 . . . 5 . . . 6 . . . 7 . . . 8 . . . 9 . . . 10.

Then they both spun around.

"Fill yer hand, ya yellow-bellied phone slinger!" shouted Mr. Klutz.

Both of them grabbed the phones off their belt loops and started punching in numbers frantically. Then they pointed their phones at each other and waited for one of them to ring.

"I know what you're thinkin'," Mr. Klutz said. "Did you punch in seven numbers or six? Well, to tell you the truth, in all the excitement, I kinda lost track myself. But you've gotta ask yourself one question: Do I feel lucky? Well, do ya, punk?"

And then Mr. Klutz's cell phone started playing "The Hokey Pokey."

"Noooooooooooooooooooooo!" he shouted.

"Ha-ha! Nice try, Klutz!" Mayor Hubble said, blowing on his phone. "Better luck next time. Now all the gold and gilver is *mine*. Adios, amigos! I must skedaddle."

The mayor got into his limo with his secret service agents and drove away.

For a few seconds nobody said anything. We were all in shock. Then Mr. Macky stepped forward.

"Dagnabbit!" he shouted. "That scallywag done vamoosed with our gold and gilver! If ah git mah hands on him, Ah'm a-gonna stretch that no-good outlaw's neck! Come on, fellers! We'll head 'im off at the pass! Who's with me?"

"No thanks," said Mrs. Roopy. "I've had enough violence for the day."

"Violence is not the answer," said Miss Laney.*

"You can't solve problems with violence," said Mr. Granite.

Why is everybody always talking about violins?

"What in tarnation!" shouted Mr. Macky. "Ain't you cowpokes gonna help me chase down that varmint?"

Mr. Burke didn't look worried. He was leaning against the fence and picking his teeth with a toothpick.

---

*Unless the question is: Name a musical instrument with four strings.

"Hold your horses, pardner," he said. "Let the old coot go."

"Let him go?" asked Mr. Macky. "Why? What about the gilver?"

"Gilver?" said Mr. Burke. "Ain't no such thing as gilver. Ah made that stuff up. Gilver is just shiny pieces of glass I scattered around the playground."

"What about the gold?" asked Mr. Macky.

"Painted rocks," said Mr. Burke. "They ain't worth a plugged nickel."

"So you planned all this, Mr. Burke?" asked Mr. Klutz. "Why?"

"Oh, Ah figgered the mayor don't care a lick 'bout balancin' no budget," he said.

"He just wants to get rid of stuff he don't like: art, music, teachers, schools. So Ah planted that gold and gilver in the playground. Ah figgered it was only a matter of time before that greedy bunko artist would try to snatch it. The cops'll pick him up soon enough."

Well, that's pretty much what happened. The police tracked Mayor Hubble down and took him to jail. Maybe he'll be there for the rest of his life. Maybe we'll raise enough money to bring back the art and music programs. Maybe all the men will shave their beards and stop saying "Yee-ha." Maybe everybody will stop talking

about violins. Maybe they'll turn the
water fountains back on and put toilet
paper in the bathrooms again. Maybe

we'll get the monkey bars back from Rent-A-Monkey Bars. Maybe the teachers will get to keep the hot tub that isn't in the teachers' lounge. Maybe Mr. Klutz and Mr. Burke will fight on the seesaws. Maybe I'll become a principal and toast marshmallows. Maybe cannibal zombies will come out of the Underground Railroad and eat our brains. Maybe there will be a TV channel that shows nothing but stuff being blown up all day long. Maybe they'll be able to fill the big hole in the playground.

But it won't be easy, pardner!